GREYSON'S SHOES

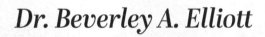

Dr. Beverley A. Elliott

Illustrator: Anna M. Costello

FriesenPress

Suite 300 - 990 Fort St
Victoria, BC, V8V 3K2
Canada

www.friesenpress.com

ISBN
978-1-5255-8887-7 (Hardcover)
978-1-5255-8886-0 (Paperback)
978-1-5255-8888-4 (eBook)

1. JUVENILE FICTION, FAMILY, PARENTS

Distributed to the trade by The Ingram Book Company

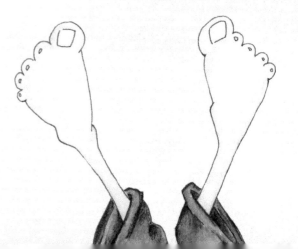

DEDICATION

To Greyson, my sweet, charming, and complex grandson. Our understanding of autism is still frighteningly limited, but if we could experience the view through the window of your world, there is so much we could learn. May life be always kind and loving to you.

Love, Grammie

I sat in my garden
Just wanting to play.
I **took off** my shoes...
They got in my way.

Along came my dad
Just doing **yard** stuff.

Off he trotted,
Pushing the mower.

I looked at my shoes...
They made me run slower.

So off they came
And flew in the air,

Onto the **table**

And then the **lawn chair.**

MY DAD HEARD
THE SOUND
HE TURNED
RIGHT
AROUND.

Over he marched
Looking so stern,
"Greyson" he said,
"I'll make you learn.
Put on those shoes
Do it right now!"

I just **looked** at him.
I didn't **know** how.

He **grabbed** my foot
And then **my leg.**
On went my shoe
Like a can on **a peg.**

Snap went the velcro,
It felt kind of tight.
I held back my laughter,
It took all my might.

Dad turned around
He stomped away.

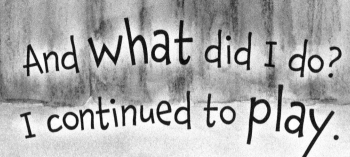

And **what** did I do?
I continued to **play**.

DARN THESE SHOES,
THEY GET IN MY WAY!

So off they came
And to my delight,
My ten tiny piggies
Enjoyed the sunlight.

HERE COMES
MY DAD
BOY!
HE LOOKS MAD!

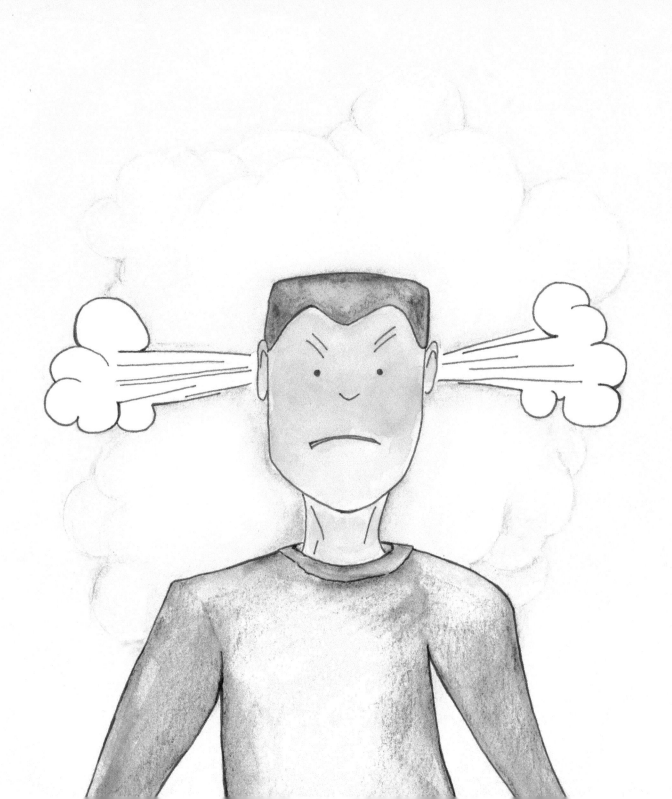

His face was all puffy
And purple and red.
I think there was steam
Coming out of his head.

"You're putting your shoes on
And there they must stay.
You won't take them off
For the rest of the day!"

On went my shoes
The Velcro it snapped.
Out came the tape
It pinched as it wrapped.

Around each shoe
And ankle it went.
The tape got all wrinkled,
One ankle looked bent.

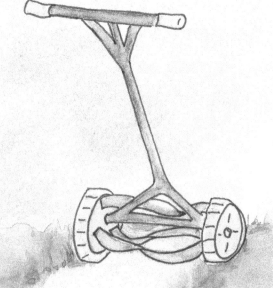

And there were my **shoes**
Not looking so neat.
My shoes looked like **boots**
With **no sign** of my feet.

I **tried** to run
But stuck to the **grass.**

It just **wasn't** fair,
Can't let this pass.

I threw off my hat,
Then tore off my shirt.
I sat in my sandbox
All covered in dirt.

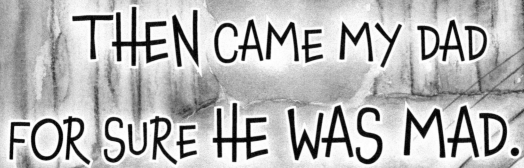

THEN CAME MY DAD
FOR SURE HE WAS MAD.

He had the tape
He picked up my hat,
Then onto my head
As quickly as that.

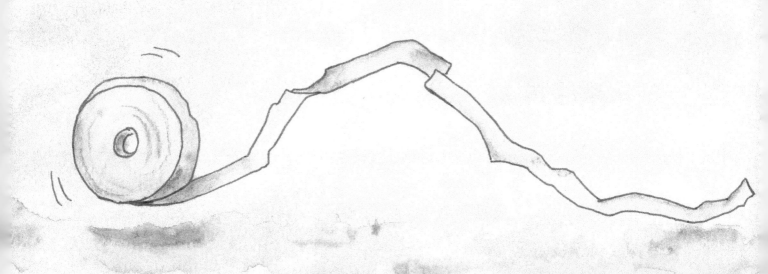

Next came my shirt
Taped onto my chest...
Then dad started laughing
And trying his best
To keep a straight face...
But he started to roll

Down on the grass

And out of control

He still had the tape
Held **tight** in his hand,
Attached to me
By a **long sticky band.**

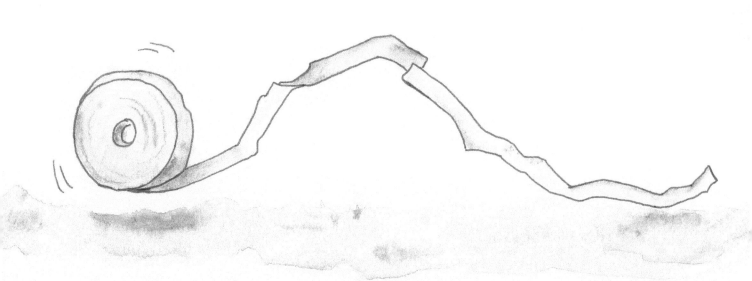

In a **couple** of rolls
I'd caught up to dad.

I got **stuck** to him
But he wasn't mad.

Dad laughed so loud
That I started giggling.
The two of us
were jiggling and wiggling.
we rolled in the yard

We were
such a sight.

We laughed **all day**
And **into** the night.

ABOUT THE AUTHOR

Children have always been the focus of my personal and professional life. In my early years, I was a pediatric nurse, then pursued a career in Medicine as a Primary Care and Consulting Pediatrician, initially in Burlington, Ont. and then Roswell, NM until I retired and returned to Canada. My heart and soul went into providing the best possible care to infants and children of all ages. Some days brought extreme challenges, some brought heartache and sadness, but mostly there was fun and laughter in the day to day interactions with my charming patients and dedicated staff. Now, through writing for young children, I hope to have a positive impact on early learning and loving to read. Words and illustrations can captivate, stimulate, and entertain endlessly, and it is to this end that I begin my new journey.

ABOUT THE ILLUSTRATOR

Anna M. Costello is a watercolor and relief-print artist and illustrator living on Vancouver Island. Her journey into illustration began when she happily noticed her evolving artwork and love of illustrations in children's books start to overlap and organically merge. Study in character design and illustrating for children only flamed the spark of curiosity and enthusiasm she found herself having for this art form. It was this discovery that lead her onto this continuing path of adventures in illustrating for children.

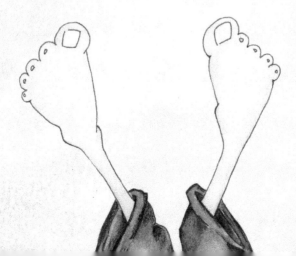

CPSIA information can be obtained
at www.ICGtesting.com
Printed in the USA
LVHW011217100221
678812LV00005B/23

9 781525 588860